For my family

Ervine, Lola and Boukie

First published 1984 by Walker Books Ltd
17-19 Hanway House, Hanway Place
London W1P 9DL

© 1984 E.J. Taylor

First printed 1984
Printed and bound in Italy by L.E.G.O., Vicenza

British Library Cataloguing in Publication Data
Taylor, E.J.
Goose eggs. — (Biscuit, Buttons and Pickles)
I. Title   II. Series
823'.914 [J]   PZ7
ISBN 0-7445-0138-5

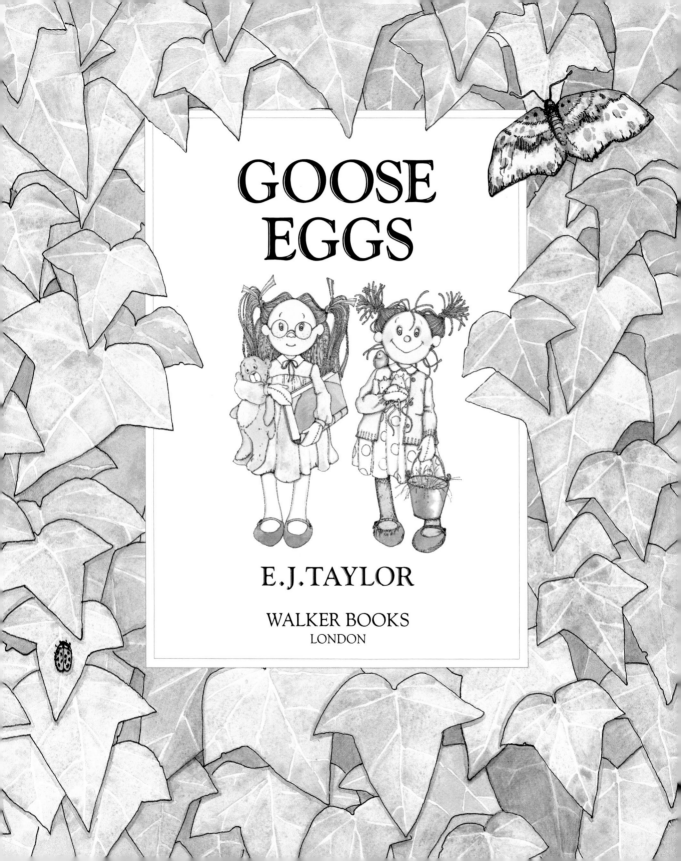

GOOSE EGGS

E.J.TAYLOR

WALKER BOOKS

LONDON

GOOSE EGGS

Ruby Buttons yawned and rubbed her eyes. She could hear the crackling of fire in the wood stove downstairs. Miss Biscuit had been awake for some time and the smells of breakfast were floating up to the bedroom. Violet was still sleeping so Ruby dressed quietly and tip-toed down to the kitchen.

'Good morning, Ruby. Did you sleep well?'

'Oh, yes, thank you.'

'Good. Then have some breakfast and you can help me look for a goat. Would you like marmalade or strawberry jam?'

Ruby looked puzzled. 'Strawberry jam, please. You mean there is a goat hiding here in the kitchen?'

Miss Biscuit laughed. 'Oh, no. Let me explain. I'm looking for a goat to buy.' And she read aloud from the newspaper. ' "Livestock auction Saturday at Duff's Farm." We're in luck, Ruby. That's today. Finish your breakfast and I'll wake Violet.'

Suddenly they heard loud screams coming from the bedroom. It was Violet and she sounded hysterical.

Miss Biscuit dropped the newspaper and ran upstairs to the bedroom. Ruby hurried behind her. Violet was standing in the middle of her bed screaming her head off.

'Violet, what on earth is the matter?'

'There's a mouse in my bed!'

'Oh dear,' said Ruby, 'I think she means Oliver.'

Ruby pulled back the blankets and picked up a small grey mouse who seemed to be even more frightened than Violet.

'This is Oliver. I found him in the garden. He's got a sore throat, so I'm keeping him inside until he feels better.'

Ruby put the tiny mouse into the pocket of her dress. 'I'm very sorry he frightened you, Violet.'

'Well, I should hope so. Mice are dirty, you know, and they don't belong inside the house.'

'There's nothing to be frightened of,' said Miss Biscuit. 'I'm sure Oliver is a very clean little mouse. Now hurry and get dressed, Violet. We're going to buy a goat today.'

They followed the footpath along the river to Farmer Duff's. A large crowd had already gathered in the barnyard. There were farm animals of every kind: horses and pigs, cows and sheep and several different goats, but Ruby said they lacked personality. They were just about to give up when Miss Biscuit spotted Matilda.

Ruby gasped. 'She must be the most beautiful brown and white goat in the world!'

And Miss Biscuit had to agree. Even Violet thought Matilda was special.

They found seats inside the barn and waited for Matilda, who was number 25, to come into the ring.

She finally appeared and when the bidding was over, Miss Biscuit had gone far over her budget for a goat. She believed, however, that extravagance was sometimes a good thing if you really had your heart set on something.

They found Matilda tied to a fence, next to her previous owner, Mrs Willoughby. But when they tried to take Matilda away, she wouldn't move. They tried everything they could to coax her, but she was determined, and refused to take a single step in any direction.

'I was afraid this would happen,' said Mrs Willoughby. 'It's Hannah, you see. Hannah is her best friend, bless her little heart. She won't go anywhere without Hannah.'

'Oh dear,' said Miss Biscuit. 'What should we do? I don't think we need two goats.'

'Why don't you have a look at her? Wait right here and I'll go and get her.'

Mrs Willoughby returned seconds later. 'This is Hannah,' she said.

'A goose!' cried Violet.

'That's right,' said Mrs Willoughby. 'Oh, and there is just one other thing.'

'What's that?' said Violet.

'Well, it's James. James and Hannah Honk — they're a pair. I wouldn't separate them for the world.'

'Oh, I see,' said Miss Biscuit. 'We'd better have a look then.'

Hannah was beautiful but James was irresistible, so Miss Biscuit and Mrs Willoughby settled the accounts for the two geese and said goodbye with a handshake.

Ruby led Matilda on a rope and James and Hannah followed Miss Biscuit along the footpath by the river back to Ivy Cottage. Violet was a little frightened of the geese and kept a safe distance behind them.

They had just passed Fern Hill when Miss Biscuit suggested they stop and rest under a large willow tree. The sun was very hot and the cool shade was a welcome relief. Matilda found some long grass and James and Hannah jumped in the water for a swim. Miss Biscuit took off her cardigan and leaned against the tree. Violet was brushing the dust off her shoes when she spotted a large green frog sitting in the tall grass next to Ruby.

'Ruby,' she whispered. 'Do not move. Do not even breathe. There is a large . . . green . . .'

The frog leaped forward. Violet screamed and ran behind a tree.

'Poor thing!' said Ruby. 'He's jumping in circles!' And she knelt down and picked up the frog.

'Ruby!' cried Violet. 'How can you touch a horrible frog?'

'He needs help. He's hurt his leg so he can't jump straight. I'm taking him home.'

Miss Biscuit agreed, over-ruling Violet's objections.

When they got home, Ruby made a splint for the frog's leg. She named him Zachary and he slept in a hat under her bed.

Ruby and Matilda became good friends and soon there was a fresh supply of milk each morning for breakfast.

In the afternoons, they all worked in the garden. Miss Biscuit took care of the weeding, Ruby did the watering and Violet was in charge of the strawberry patch. She believed that if the strawberries did not look good, they would not taste good. She spent hours polishing each leaf with warm water and a soft cloth, until they were all bright and shiny.

On very hot days they would pack a lunch and go for a picnic along the river near Fern Hill.

Ruby had several new pets to look after and seemed to find some tiny creature in need of help wherever she went. Miss Biscuit was busy making jars and jars of preserves from the garden and Violet was reading the complete works of Shakespeare.

The summer days passed quietly with their routine changing very little, until one very hot day at the end of July.

Miss Biscuit and Violet were preparing dinner when Ruby pushed open the kitchen door.

'You must come at once,' she said in an excited voice.

'What is it?' asked Miss Biscuit.

'It's a surprise,' said Ruby, 'I can't tell you.'

Ruby turned and raced out of the kitchen. Miss Biscuit and Violet followed her, running all the way down to the river.

'Oh, for heaven's sake,' said Miss Biscuit. 'She's built a nest.'

'Yes,' said Ruby, 'and guess what else! She has five eggs! I want to move her up to the bedroom where she'll be safe . . .'

Violet did not wait for Ruby to finish.

'ABSOLUTELY NOT!'

'But Violet,' said Ruby, 'there are wild animals all along the river at night. It's dangerous.'

'There are wild animals all over the bedroom!' replied Violet. 'Baby squirrels in the stocking drawer, a turtle and a frog under the bed, a robin in the sewing basket and yesterday I found a mole sleeping in my shoe box. If that goose comes into the house I'm leaving!' Violet stomped her foot and marched back to the cottage.

'Oh dear,' said Ruby. 'Now what will I do?'

Miss Biscuit took Ruby's hand. 'There isn't a problem in the world that can't be solved — you'll think of something. Now let's eat some dinner.'

That night after dinner
Ruby walked out to the big
oak tree and sat in the
swing. A light wind was
blowing. Ruby moved back
and forth, lost in her thoughts.
'What am I going to do?'
She held on to the ropes
and leaned back so far that she
could see high into the tree.
'A tree house!' she said.
'I'll build a tree house
for the animals.
Oh what a good idea!'
And she hurried inside to
tell Violet and Miss Biscuit.

A few hours after they had gone to bed, a light rain began to fall. In a short time, the wind grew stronger and the rain became so heavy that the noise woke Ruby as it pounded against her window. She sat up.

'Hannah's out there in all this rain!' she cried and jumped out of bed.

Miss Biscuit was in the hall by the linen cupboard collecting blankets and towels. 'Take this basket,' she said to Ruby, 'and follow me.' They rushed downstairs and out the front door toward the river.

Hannah was cold and shivering but she hadn't moved from her nest. Miss Biscuit wrapped her in a blanket. Ruby carefully laid her eggs in the basket and they ran back to the cottage.

Violet was waiting by the front door with more towels. They soon had Hannah dry and Ruby put her eggs in a box of straw by the warm stove in the kitchen. Hannah quickly returned to her nest, still shivering but safely out of the rain.

Miss Biscuit put some wood on the fire and they all went back to bed.

The next morning it had stopped raining but the sky looked grey and unfriendly. They woke up early and hurried down to the kitchen. Hannah was still shivering even though she was wrapped in a warm blanket.

Miss Biscuit felt under Hannah's wing. 'This doesn't look good,' she said. 'I'm afraid she's caught a chill.'

'Will she be all right?' said Ruby.

'I think so,' replied Miss Biscuit, 'but I am concerned about her eggs. I think we had better get the hot water bottles.'

They watched Hannah closely for the rest of the afternoon, changing the hot water bottles almost every hour. By the evening she was shivering so badly that she had difficulty staying on her nest.

Miss Biscuit sat close by stroking her head. 'Poor Hannah,' she sighed.

Ruby added another blanket and patted her gently.

Violet burst into tears. 'It's all my fault!' she cried, and ran quickly up the stairs.

Violet lay on her bed and cried so hard that her pillow was soon soaked with tears. By the time Miss Biscuit knocked on the door she had the hiccups as well.

'C-C-C-C-Come in-n-n-n,' she sobbed.

Miss Biscuit walked into the bedroom. Ruby followed. 'Please don't cry, Violet,' said Ruby in a soft voice.

Violet sobbed louder. 'But it's my fault Hannah's sick.'

'It's not your fault,' said Miss Biscuit. 'None of us knew it was going to rain. We can't help Hannah with tears.'

Violet sat up. 'You're right,' she said with a sniff. 'I must think of a way to help.'

'That's better,' said Miss Biscuit. 'Now we must get back to the kitchen. It's time to change the hot water bottle.'

Ruby kissed Violet on the cheek and followed Miss Biscuit.

Violet jumped off the bed, ran to her book shelf and found a large, brown leather book. She opened it and began to read. 'Herbs and Country Medicines.'

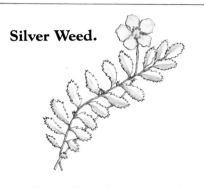

Silver Weed.

Also called Goose Weed.
Brew tea with leaves. Good
for general health of geese.

By the time she reached page 176, Violet was becoming just a little discouraged. 'Silver Weed,' she read aloud, and paused.

She looked at the drawing. 'I've seen this growing near Fern Hill,' she said.

Violet ran to the window. It was dark outside and it had started to rain again. She put on a raincoat, tip-toed down the stairs and slipped out the front door.

Fern Hill was some distance from Ivy Cottage. It was also a frightening journey in the dark.

'I must be brave,' she said out loud, 'and I won't think about wild animals that prowl in the night.'

The rain grew harder and the wind was howling. Violet continued, keeping step to the squashing sound of wet stocking inside her shoes. 'I won't be afraid, I won't be afraid,' she said over and over.

It seemed like hours but she reached Fern Hill and found the spot where they came for picnics. The patch of goose weed was close by. Violet picked as much as she could carry and started back home.

Miss Biscuit and Ruby were still in the kitchen when Violet returned.

'Violet!' cried Miss Biscuit. 'Where have you been?'

Violet explained what she had done as Miss Biscuit helped to take off her wet clothes. Ruby brought her a dry bathrobe. When she had changed, Violet made the goose weed tea for Hannah. Miss Biscuit fed it to her with a large soup spoon and in a short time Hannah stopped shivering and fell asleep.

In a few days she had recovered completely.

Ruby began to build
her tree house, and Violet helped in
every way she could. When they finished,
Miss Biscuit painted a sign. After all the
animals had been moved safely from the
bedroom to the tree house, they hung
the sign over the door. It read:
RUBY BUTTONS' ANIMAL HOSPITAL.

The leaves were beginning to fade and the nights were growing cooler. Summer was coming to an end. Miss Biscuit, Ruby and Violet worked every day gathering vegetables from the garden.

They had picked the beans, pulled the carrots and on the morning they were starting to dig the potatoes, James and Hannah arrived at the back door with five newly-hatched baby geese. They were very proud of their new family and so were Ruby and Violet.

It had been a happy summer for everyone, thanks to some quick thinking, some very hard work and five lovely goose eggs.